WINGS OF DESTINY

UNIVERSE IN FLAMES (BOOK 0)

CHRISTIAN KALLIAS

SHORT FOREWORD

Wings of Destiny can be considered **Universe in Flames'** book 0.

It happens before the events of **Earth - Last Sanctuary**. It follows the series protagonist while he's in the Star Alliance pilot's academy.

It is chronologically the first book in the series, and it's as good a place to start as book 1, although **Earth - Last Sanctuary** is the first book that was created in this universe (so it's also a good starting point). **Wings of Destiny** was written in Spring 2018 after the entire first series (or season) was written. It's not required reading but I do hope you enjoy reading it as much as I have enjoyed writing it.

It's also an homage to both **Top Gun** & **Wing Commander**, respectively my favorite movie & video game growing up.

It was never released to Amazon before it was included in

the Ultimate box set Edition. Now you can read it on its own for the first time, with a brand new cover and the latest sets of edits.

ACKNOWLEDGMENTS

Cover artwork by Christian Kallias

- christian@kallias.com
- www.christiankallias.com
- www.facebook.com/ChristianKallias
- www.twitter.com/kalliasx

Production Editor & Alpha/ARC Team Lead

- Paula Lavattiata Lopez

Editors

- Paula Lavattiata Lopez

Proofreaders

- Paula Lavattiata Lopez
- Alpha Readers

COPYRIGHT

Copyright © 2021 by Christian Kallias

First Printing, 2018

Version 1.12

ALSO BY CHRISTIAN KALLIAS

—== Access All my Books Here ==—

christiankallias.com

The Universe in Flames Series

- Book 1: Earth - Last Sanctuary (Definitive Edition)
- Book 1.5: Ryonna's Wrath (Novella)
- Book 2: Fury to the Stars
- Book 3: Destination Oblivion
- Book 4: The Beginning of the End
- Book 5: Rise of the Ultra Fury
- Book 6: Shadows of Olympus

- Book 7: Armageddon Unleashed
- Book 8: Twilight of the Gods
- Book 9: Requiem of Souls
- Book 10: To End All Wars (Final Chapter)
- Book 11: Nemesis
- Book 12: Unleashed
- Book 13: Reckoning
- Book 14: Dominion
- Book 15: Fireborn (releases October 2021)
- *Books 1-13 also available in trilogies format.*

Universe In Flames - Origins

- Episode 1: Course Correction
- Episode 2: Damocles Fall
- Wings of Destiny (*this book*)

Far Beyond Series

- Book 0: Across the Galactic Pond
- Book 1: Fire At Will
- Book 2: Make it So!
- Book 3: Battlestations
- *The complete series is available in a box set with an extra story (Book 2.5) called Red Alert.*

Rewind Series

- Book 0: Out of Time (Collateral Damage anthology)
- Book 1: Freedom's End
- Book 2: Pandemonium
- Book 3: Nightfall

- **Galactic Tales** (10 Epic Stories from Earth & Beyond)

Sign up for my newsletter to keep up to date with new releases and promotions.

1

This story takes place thousands of light-years away from Earth. In a part of space where the Star Alliance and the Obsidian Empire have been waging a war for generations.

The missile grazed Chase's ship, briefly illuminating his cockpit in a radiant blue before it reacquired its lock.

"Missile lock," said AINI, the onboard navicomputer AI.

"No shit!" exclaimed Chase. "You're really a stickler for stating the obvious."

"I'm sorry, Pilot, I do not understand your last command."

The AI's vocal sub-routines made the female computer's voice sound like a mixture of artificial calm and unintended digital sexiness. Something that Chase found, more often than not, disconcerting.

Chase exhaled in frustration. He would have to find an engineer cadet willing to sacrifice some of his spare time to give the ship's AI a much-needed personality boost. Chase made a mental note of it as his ship's proximity alert started blaring, informing him the missile was once more on his tailpipe and ready to impact with his weak shields.

"Never mind that, AINI, divert all power to the shields and execute evasive pattern Theta-3."

"Executing," said AINI.

As the missile gained on him, Chase spun his ship one hundred and eighty degrees on its Z axis and took back manual control. He locked onto the missile with his lasers, set them to rapid fire, and blasted it into oblivion.

"Three more enemy ships on approach vector," warned AINI.

Of course they are.

"Power redirected," added AINI, "shield at sixty-two percent and rising."

Chase took a second to look at his instruments to assess the situation as well as the status of his ordnance. He only had a pair of missiles left, which wasn't ideal. He'd have to make do.

The moment the enemy ships entered firing range, Chase veered his ship hard, vectoring toward the trio of incoming fighters. Red laser fire screamed past his canopy and briefly illuminated his cockpit with crimson tones. Chase flew his fighter in a corkscrew maneuver, trying to avoid as many hits as possible until he was ready to make his move.

The enemy ships flew in a tight pyramid formation. The corner of Chase's mouth arched into a grin. He locked onto the apex craft as more laser fire pounded and depleted his frontal shields at an alarming rate. He fired his first missile, then almost immediately after, fired a second one at the same target. The first missile lit up and exploded on the enemy's shields, the follow-up pierced through them and tore the fighter's wing to shreds.

The enemy craft spun uncontrollably. Molten parts, sparks, and oxygen spewing into space. The other two ships tried to break away but one wasn't fast enough; the damaged fighter exploded on its shield, sending it spinning out of control. Chase acquired it, unwilling to let this brief window of opportunity slip through his fingers. He showered the craft with rapid bursts of low-power laser fire, making short-change of what little shields the enemy had left. Chase switched his firing mode to heavy, supercharged laser fire, aimed at the ship's engine, and blew the fighter to kingdom come.

Chase cheered as he flew through the resulting cloud of dust and debris. A few of the smaller fragments burned on his shields, bringing them down to under ten percent.

"Buy one, get one free," Chase chuckled.

But his victorious dance was interrupted when he received heavy laser fire on his starboard side. The incoming fire finished off whatever shield remained, and several hits broke pieces off his Manticore starfighter as alarm holo-controls lit up throughout his cockpit.

Dammit!

Chase went evasive. Knowing he was in trouble, his instincts fired up. He couldn't let the last ship score even a single hit more if he wanted to win this engagement.

His heart skipped a beat when a heavy pounding noise resonated from the top of the cockpit.

"Chase! Stop fooling around in that thing; we're gonna to be late for class!" Daniel shouted.

Chase refrained from swearing at his best friend.

"I just need another minute," he shouted back, with no small quantity of frustration seeping into his voice.

Chase veered away and went evasive. He had lost focus, and his mind wandered outside of the simulator. It was pure luck that the last enemy ship hadn't blown him out of the sky during that time.

"We can't be late today, buddy, remember special guest and all. Admiral Tharowni will have your ass this time."

"Leave me alone, go. I'll be right behind you."

Chase was met with silence, during which he tried to get his bearings and check the position of the enemy fighter. It had moved right into his six.

Perfect, just fucking perfect!

"Alright, buddy," said Daniel. "I'm going. See you in class."

Chase huffed but didn't answer, infuriated that his focus was interrupted from the virtual firefight. He knew Daniel meant well, but in this very moment, anger filled Chase's mind like a deadly virus, threatening his ability to fly his ship, let alone engage in a dogfight, virtual or otherwise.

He took a deep breath, trying to calm himself, and for just a split second, in the back of his mind, he thought he heard a female voice.

"Stay calm, you can do this. You can do anything you set your mind to."

Great, I'm hearing voices now, can this day get any worse?

As if in answer from the universe, part of Chase's wing splintered as the remaining enemy fighter scored three laser hits.

Son of a bit—

Unfortunately, Chase's attempt to remain calm failed. His muscles tightened, and he began to sweat, his anger turning to rage and spreading within his body like venom coursing through his veins. Then, something happened, and it felt as if time were slowing down, giving Chase a reprieve to check out the situation and find a way out of his current predicament that didn't involve him losing this fight.

Above all else, Chase hated to lose.

He tried to redistribute power to the shields, but the generators were damaged. He would have to finish this dogfight without them.

So be it!

Chase evaded the next wave of laser fire, dodging, rolling, and sliding through space like a sinuous sea eel on a mission, even with a damaged wing, never letting the enemy fire come close to scoring a hit. His focus was now back one hundred percent, to the point that the dogfight felt real to Chase, and he had to win as if his life depended on it.

It took some doing, but Chase eventually managed to line up his fighter into the bandit's six o'clock position and finally had the enemy ship in his visor.

You're mine now!

Chase got a nice lock tone, only to be reminded by the ships' AI that he no longer had any missiles. Was it her condescending tone or just Chase's annoyance at forgetting something so obvious, he didn't know. But he redirected the AI's power to the weapons, effectively disabling any future vocal messages from AINI.

Now, where was I?

The enemy starfighter started jinking, but Chase was determined to shoot it out of the sky by any means necessary. He stuck on its six no matter what, continuously pounding the enemy's aft shields; however, the levels were dropping too slowly.

Chase checked his power readings only to notice that he had lost power to the laser cannon located on his damaged wing. It had sprung a power leak. Chase whipped his head to the side and saw sparks fly from the flaming wing every time he took a shot. This was unfortunate as his ship could blow up if he continued to ignore the leak.

Inhaling deeply, Chase tried calming his mind, which was on the brink of blowing a fuse.

I love a challenge, he recited as a mantra.

Chase's hands blurred on the holo-controls as he redistributed all power to the functioning cannon, bypassing the power node on the damaged wing altogether.

That cost him precious seconds during which the enemy fighter, still unable to shake Chase off his tail, managed to recharge most of its shields.

I've lost enough time dancing around with you, say your prayers to whichever digital gods you believe in.

Chase felt as if he entered a trance. He switched his laser to full power, siphoning as much energy from literally every system in order to supercharge the one working cannon to one hundred and forty percent. Every one of his supercharged shots hit the enemy ship, draining its shield rapidly. Two more hits and its shields went down. Sparks flew from one of the damaged engines. It was losing speed.

"Time to say goodbye now—"

Chase depressed the trigger on his flight stick to take the winning shot, but nothing happened. Another three red status indicators illuminated on his holo-controls.

You've got to be shitting me.

Chase twitched. *It ain't no thing. You want to play it this way, then let's fucking play.*

Bolstered with an inhuman influx of motivation, Chase's mind took over, and he felt as if he were watching a holo-movie, as if some strange force was taking over his actions and left him only as a witness. He redirected all power to the engines, even life support, and pushed through at full burn. With the extra juice in his engines and the enemy slowing down, Chase accelerated on a collision course and approached his prey fast. Very fast. He disregarded the "collision imminent" alert.

Here goes nothing.

A split second before he would have rammed into the enemy fighter, Chase rolled his Manticore ninety degrees and vectored his nose just below the enemy, using his good wing to cut at the belly of his prey like gutting a fish. Metal ground, sparks and flames flew, and every warning and alarm inside Chase's cockpit lit up at once on his holo-controls. With AINI down, the alarms were displayed as hovering holo-text.

"Ship structural integrity failure imminent, ejecting pilot now!"

His pilot chair was spinning in space as he saw the last scene unfold.

The enemy ship was nearly cut in half by Chase's crazy stunt, but by some miracle, it was still flying, somewhat. Chase's ship, on the other hand, blew up into multiple fiery displays of explosions behind the enemy ship, incinerating it in the process.

"I win!" he exclaimed as the holo-projectors reset and the simulator cockpit latch opened. Chase jumped out of the machine to an empty mess hall. Nobody to applaud his last crazy display, and nobody giving their constructive criticism as to how insane his fighting style was and how they wished they would never have to fly with him in a real combat situation.

Hell, even the barman had left the premises.

"Ooookay," said Chase.

He looked at his wrist holo-device and saw the hour. He was more than ten minutes late for class.

I'm in trouble, he thought as he darted toward section three of the space station.

2

"How generous of you to grace us with your presence, Cadet Athanatos!" bellowed the teacher, Admiral Tharowni.

Chase waved his hand timidly. "Sorry, Admiral," he said as he sat behind Daniel. "I— I was detained, well, sort of. It won't happen again," he added with an unconvincing smile.

"I don't care what excuse you think you can cook up this time, Cadet! I have half a mind to ask you to leave. And today of all days, you could have made an effort. Let me be perfectly clear, this is your *last* warning. If you ever arrive at my class late again from now until the end of the year, you can kiss your days at the academy goodbye. Is that understood?"

That's a little rough, take it easy old fart, Chase thought.

"What did you just say?" asked the admiral.

Chase swallowed hard. Had he voiced his inner thoughts without realizing?

Chase quickly glanced around and could tell from the many baffled looks that he wasn't the only one surprised. If he somehow had been heard, he would be in big trouble, so he stood up straight, swallowed his pride, and saluted.

"I'm sorry, Admiral. As per your question: understood through and through! Thank you for giving me one last chance, you won't regret it."

Chase thought he heard a classmate from the other side of the classroom whisper "sucker."

The admiral threw his hands in Chase's direction. "Shut up, Cadet, and sit the hell back down. Oh, and today, just for once, try and learn something, okay? It's not every day that you are exposed to a living, breathing war hero."

Chase sat back in his chair, releasing a long and silent exhale of relief.

I'm surprised you're not including yourself in that statement today.

Chase grinned. "Will do, sir."

The Admiral was notorious for recounting his glory days during class and putting himself on a pedestal, which annoyed Chase to no end. For a moment he wondered why that was until Daniel turned his head slightly to the side and whispered.

"I hope your joyride in the simulator was worth getting your last blemish. One more cock-up and they'll fire your ass. Who will I hang around with if you get your dumb ass fired from this place?"

Your concern is touching. You're lucky you're my best friend, or I'd kick your ass.

While Chase wanted to argue with his friend that the admiral was probably just bluffing, weirdly, his instincts told him otherwise. Though he shouldn't be surprised, he had, after all, repeatedly been late, disobedient, and sometimes just plain distracted to the point where dismissal from the academy was probably a real possibility. Now was definitely not the right time to attract more attention to himself.

The thought of being dismissed did scare Chase more than he thought it would. Was it his love of flying that would die should he not finish and graduate from the academy? Most likely, but something else at the back of his mind screamed at him that he had to stop screwing around and take his classes a little more seriously.

"I'll tell you about it later," Chase whispered back. "Better not anger the dragon."

Daniel turned his head even more and gave Chase a befuddled look that spoke more than any words could.

"Now it's time to present the esteemed guest of the day," said Tharowni. "Class, attention!"

Everyone got up as the admiral walked to the door. It split open and revealed a bearded man with an iron look in his eyes. He wore a captain's uniform, and even though Chase was far, he could read the name of the ship under his slew of medals.

The *Destiny*.

"Class, it is my privilege to introduce you to Captain Saroudis. Hero of the battle of the Thermopylae Pulsar. I'm sure you all know about it by now. It's been all over the holo-news for the past month."

Chase had indeed read about it. Captain Adonis Saroudis had used cunning strategy and tactics to defeat a much bigger and more powerful fleet. He had waged battle for three days, relentlessly, and had sent whatever was left of the Obsidian Empire forces packing.

A round of applause filled the room.

Captain Saroudis scanned the classroom and permitted himself a small smile.

"Thank you, Cadets," said Saroudis. "As you were."

Everyone sat back down.

"Thank you, Admiral, for having me here. It's an honor."

"The honor is ours."

The admiral whispered something in the captain's ear, and he nodded slightly before taking a couple of steps forward, looking straight out at the class.

"The admiral would like me to give you a bit of a motivational speech. I wish I could say that your training here will prepare you for what awaits you once you graduate and are assigned to your destroyer carrier in a few months. Perhaps even on board my own ship.

"Unfortunately, I can't and won't lie to you. War is ugly, it's tough, and it will make your life miserable more often than not, that is if you survive it."

Chase could tell from Admiral Tharowni's uneasy face that the captain's words were not what he had in mind for a motivational speech. But the words resonated with Chase, so Saroudis had his undivided attention.

"You see," continued Saroudis. "This conflict has been going on for generations, my father, heck, even my grandfather, have been involved in it. I lost them both to this bloody war. In fact, I was very young when my grandfather's starfighter was destroyed during the onslaught at the battle of Dervenakia."

The captain's face hardened before he continued.

"Such is war. You lose people. In fact, you're very likely to lose your own life. I can see on some of your faces that this isn't what you wanted to hear today. And I'm sorry if I'm bringing your spirits down. It's not my intention, but I don't like lying to anybody, let alone young minds that are training to defend the Star Alliance and what we stand for. I owe it to you to tell you what war really is and what you're going to have to expect in the career you have chosen.

"Like you, I've been through the academy, I flew simulators, then proper live training missions until I was finally assigned to a wing onboard my father's ship, the *Argolis*. Had my father requested my presence? Or was it just the luck of the draw? I never found the courage to ask him the question for fear of learning something I didn't want to know. And so I was there, in my fighter's cockpit, shot to hell, my engines on fire, when both my father and his ship exploded into a million pieces."

The class had never been this silent. The cold, hard reality check Saroudis painted with such eloquence, was filled with deep emotional backwash that he managed, for the most part, to not let impact either his tone or the message he was trying to convey to the young people's minds in attendance.

"No. I can't lie to you," continued Saroudis. "I won't. That moment was, without a doubt, the most excruciatingly painful one of my entire existence. It still hurts today. But it was also a defining moment for me. Even though a part of me died when I saw my father's ship explode, and at that moment I felt like giving up, and for a handful of seconds, thought about letting the enemy finish me off and put me out of my misery. My fighter was shot to hell, barely still flying, shields failing, half of my power nodes fluctuating. But if I had, then thousands of courageous men, my father included, would have lost their lives in vain. They were fighting for a cause, and that day I realized that so was I, so I couldn't give up. I patched up my fighter and kept fighting, and so did the rest of my wing until we drove the Empire away from our space."

There was a long silence.

"This is what war will do to you. But without the sacrifices of brave men and woman, we may not keep our freedom, and could end up being squashed under the Obsidian Empire's tyranny. So we wage war, fighting and dying for the Star Alliance at a moment's notice if that is our destiny. For that, I want to thank you for being here, for willing to put your lives in jeopardy for what you believe in. I may have brought your spirits down a little today, but I know that in each of your hearts flows the blood of warriors. Heroes of tomorrow. We need you, more than you realize."

Chase was the first to get up and clap, and the rest of the class followed suit. The entire speech struck a chord with him, and for the first time in a long time, he actually felt like he was in the right place, doing the right thing. This feeling would fade away later that day when he and the captain would clash on tactics. But, for now, Chase was perfectly happy to bask in the moment. Little did he know this would be a pivotal moment that would shape his future.

3

Chase destroyed the last of the enemy fighters with barely any of his shields left before the simulation ended. He removed the neural interface from his temple. This advanced piece of technology was still in its beta stages and sometimes glitchy, though Chase had to admit that the engineers in charge of its development were working out the kinks at an impressive pace the last few months. The neural implant projected a virtual holographic scene directly inside the mind of its wearer. It was, in fact, just like a regular simulator, except it weighed almost nothing and could link with other minds to practice both standalone and networked dogfight scenarios or even full squadron maneuvers like he just did with his classmates.

Chase looked around, his classmates staring at him. Some looked surprised, some cast him disapproving glances, very few seemed to glean some sort of inspiration from him. Or so it seemed to Chase.

"Alright," said Saroudis. "Who can tell me what Cadet Athanatos did wrong?"

Wrong? I just killed four fighters!

For a moment Chase thought Daniel would raise his hand, but Fillio beat him to it. Fillio Steriopoulou was another of Chase's friends, though there was more to their relationship than that, even though Chase didn't know where they were headed with it just yet. It was against regulations to date another fellow pilot.

Like with every other rule, Chase didn't like that particular one.

"Yes, Cadet," said Saroudis as he pointed toward Fillio.

"He broke off and abandoned his wingman in the middle of the fight."

No kiss for you later today, Chase thought.

"However," Fillio added, "he did take down four enemy fighters pretty much on his own."

Chase smiled. *On the other hand...*

"That part was impressive, but that doesn't excuse the fact that he left his wingman hanging high and dry," countered Saroudis. "Sure, the cadet seems very good at breaking every rule in the book and flying by the seat of his pants. Granted, his instincts seem pretty strong. But, discipline and rules are there for a reason. Right, Mr. Athanatos?"

Chase suddenly felt everyone's eyes upon him. For a moment, he even felt like he was about to freeze. Now the question was, should he tell the captain how he felt about his question, or should he try to conform to what was expected of him as a Star Alliance pilot? For a moment Chase thought he would go with the latter, but then he remembered how he felt when Saroudis poured his heart out and told them how he lost his father. The man deserved Chase's honest answer.

"I think rules and discipline are important, I just happen to think I fly better doing my own thing, no offense."

Captain Saroudis sized up Chase for what felt like the

longest time. Chase had no idea what the next words coming from his mouth would be. If Chase's answer had generated an emotional impact on the captain, he wasn't letting it show. Not one iota, in fact.

"That's a better answer than I expected you to give, Cadet. And I appreciate that you didn't just cow down and agree with me when your flying clearly displays that you are, indeed, doing your own thing. Now class, while the cadet seems to fly well with his instincts, let me tell you why you shouldn't try to emulate him and why you'd rather have someone who flies by the book as your wingman."

Chase flinched. There had been some tempered compliments behind the captain's words, and he didn't completely shut him down like he was used to with Admiral Tharowni. Still, not exactly an endorsement of his flight skills either.

We'll see about that wingman comment when your life will, in fact, depend on my flight skills.

Chase's attention drifted away after that, not even caring to listen to the arguments on the logic behind never abandoning one's wingman. Chase didn't care about logic; he cared and listened to his gut, and he intended to continue to do so.

Daniel swiveled in his chair and entered something on his wrist holo-device. Chase's device vibrated, and Daniel's message hovered an inch from his wrist.

"Chin up, bro. The way you killed those four bogeys was amazing."

"Thanks, buddy," Chase answered on his device.

～

AT THE END OF CLASS, as the cadets headed to their quarters, Captain Saroudis called to Chase.

"Cadet Athanatos. If I may have a moment with you."

Chase shrugged almost dismissively. "Sure, why not. What can I do for you, Captain?"

"It's more what I can do for you, Cadet."

"And what would that be?"

"I know where you're coming from, I— I've been bending the rules when push comes to shove, and more often than not, that saved many lives."

Chase squinted his eyes. "Why are you telling me this?"

"Because I recognize a fire in you. I used to have that same fire in my eyes as well as the same attitude problem."

Attitude problem, huh?

"I can tell from your reaction," continued Saroudis, "that you don't think you're the problem."

"I wouldn't go that far."

"You would if we were off the record. Which by the way, we are."

There was silence.

"Look, Cadet," Saroudis continued when it became clear that Chase wouldn't talk. "I didn't mean to give you a hard time in front of your classmates. And if I made you feel uncomfortable, well, I'm sorry. I just think you need to curb some of that pride that shines through your entire personality. You're young, inexperienced, and if I may speak frankly—"

Chase nodded.

"You're unprepared for what's to come in the future. Blowing up digital ghost ships and actually taking lives are two different things."

Chase swallowed hard and had to restrain himself from letting the anger show in his demeanor. Saroudis put his hand on his shoulder and looked at Chase squarely in the eyes.

"There was pure genius in your flying today, but I can't acknowledge it. Not publicly. Pilots with your kind of instincts are needed, one day you'll probably do something heroic and save people's lives. But I can't encourage this behavior toward other cadets that don't have that instinct you seem to have been born with. Do you understand?"

To say that Chase had been unprepared for the captain's words would be an understatement.

"I do. Thank you for saying so."

"I also want you to know that, even though you clearly can put your money where your mouth is, you will see many roadblocks in your career in doing so. For instance, if you want to become a wing commander, or even a captain one day, you'll have to curb some of that 'fire' you have."

I just want to fly a starfighter.

"What's on your mind, Cadet? And, please, don't sugar-coat your answer."

"With all due respect, Captain. I just want to fly a Manti-core starfighter and kill as many Obsidian Empire bogeys as I can. That's all that matters to me."

Saroudis smiled. "I can say with confidence that I'm sure you'll get that done. But don't discard what else you could achieve in your lifetime." Saroudis chuckled before continuing. "I see a lot of myself in you at your age. If there's one thing I can impart to you, it is that you never know what the future holds. You may think you're just the lone wolf pilot, misunderstood, shunned by others who are in fact jealous of your innate abilities. But sooner than you might expect, the universe might serve up another kind of destiny for you, one you can't imagine right now."

Chase took some time to digest the words. He liked Saroudis, he seemed like an empathic person.

"Thank you, Captain. I—"

"Yes, Cadet? Tell me."

"I don't believe in destiny, sir. I think we make our own."

"And on some level, I'm sure you're right. But give it time, one day you might wake up and realize that destiny is knocking on your door. I've taken enough of your time, I'm sure you want to go back to your quarters and enjoy your evening."

"Thank you, Captain. I enjoyed this talk."

Saroudis smiled. "So did I. You're dismissed."

Chase was almost out the door when he stopped and turned around.

"How long will you be staying on Starbase Alpha Three, sir?"

"My battlegroup is scheduled to leave in a couple of days, Cadet."

"Will you be teaching more classes until then?"

"You bet, I'll see you tomorrow, Cadet."

Chase smiled and nodded before leaving the classroom.

ADMIRAL THAROWNI DESCENDED from the back of the class and came next to the captain as Chase left the room.

"He's a different fellow, this Chase," said Tharowni. "Did you talk some sense into him?"

Saroudis smiled as he brushed his hand through his well-groomed beard. "In a manner of speaking."

"Good. He sure needs to learn his place. Always late, fighting with other cadets, he's got quite a temperament."

"That I have no doubt believing, Admiral. But was I any different?"

The admiral chuckled. "I'd like to think so, yes."

"He's an excellent pilot, though."

"Not a team player, but yes, some of the maneuvers he's pulled, at least in the simulators, I've never seen anything like it. I just wish he had a slightly different attitude."

"Well, he is who he is. At least it must make your days interesting, right?"

"Oh yeah, I'm running out of ways to formulate new blemishes on his record."

Saroudis laughed.

4

____

This evening had started so well.

Daniel, Fillio, and Chase were drinking at the bar, exchanging jokes, taking friendly potshots at one another, until Cadet Luyet decided to be a smart-ass.

It wasn't the first remark where he paraphrased Saroudis and focused only on the negative from today's class. No, that one Chase had managed to let slide. Nor was it the cadet's second remark about how he would never fly on Chase's wing. Since Chase had no intention of ever inflicting himself with such an imposition, he had managed to stay calm.

No, all hell broke loose when big mouth Luyet went to no man's land.

"Listen up!" Luyet yelled to anyone within earshot. "It's obvious why our boy here, Chase, doesn't care about rules or anyone but himself. I mean, wouldn't you be a rebel too if you didn't know your heritage or being adopted at a mature age? I mean, come on, he doesn't even remember his past or the fact that he doesn't have *real* parents."

This was when the shit hit the fan.

Five minutes later, a brawl of epic proportions ravaged the mess hall, and Chase had thrown the first, lip-splitting punch. One that Luyet was unlikely to forget until it healed.

In hindsight and looking at the brig's force field, he regretted his actions. But Luyet had been out of line. Still, Chase feared that this last incident might just be the last straw that could cost him his place in the Star Alliance Academy. And today had generally been a good day, he had fun in both the simulator and listening to Captain Saroudis in class, only to cross that line that he was just starting to see in his mind. Having crossed it, he might regret it for the rest of his life.

Every minute spent in the brig felt like an eternity. Were the instructors deciding his fate right now? Would he get expelled? The thought scared the shit out of him. By the time Admiral Tharowni came to the brig, Chase felt like an entire month had passed.

He started to sweat, and he felt like he could hear his heart trying to pound its way out of his chest. He didn't like the look in the admiral's eyes.

Dammit, please, don't let this happen.

Tharowni requested the security officer to lower the force field. Once it was down, he walked in the cell, sat next to Chase, and interlocked his fingers together without saying a word.

Should I apologize now? Or wait until he speaks? Chase wondered.

When the silence became too unbearable, and Chase thought his mind would explode, he blurted.

"I fucked up, didn't I?"

Tharowni briefly glanced at Chase then returned his attention to his hands.

I did. That's it. They'll throw me out.

"I'm going to tell you a story. I'd like you to listen closely to it."

What? Why won't you tell me if I'm expelled?

"Okay," said Chase.

"I lost my birth parents in the war. I was too young to remember or understand. Fortunately, a nice couple who couldn't have children adopted me. They made me feel like their own. It was only when I reached puberty that they disclosed it to me.

"Even though I was too young to remember my real parents, I still felt betrayed. Why would they pretend to be my parents? But after a few weeks, I realized that it didn't matter whether or not they were my birth parents. They took me in, they loved me just as much as they would have their own child, and they made me feel safe.

"In the time it took for me to reach that life-altering conclusion, I had complained to a few too many of my friends, and the word got out that I was adopted."

Where is he going with this?

"I know the only thing on your mind right now must be your fate in this school. I don't want to torture you by telling you my entire, not-so-interesting, life story. And until five minutes ago, when I looked at your record, I hadn't realized something. While we share a similarity in that story, in the fact that we're both adopted, there's a divergence in our respective lives. My adoptive parents died of old age. And while I was filing the paperwork for your expulsion out of this academy, I felt compelled to check your records."

Admiral Tharowni put his hand on Chase's shoulder.

"I'm sorry you can't say the same about yours."

A single tear ran down Chase's face.

"So, I trashed the order to have you expelled because I think your reaction to the bullying from Cadet Luyet was not only understandable under the circumstances, but warranted. If I had been in your shoes, I probably would have bashed his head in too."

Chase turned toward the admiral, not knowing what to say.

"That being said," Tharowni continued, "you need to understand something, Chase. You have been a negative influence on the class, your constant tardiness, your general attitude, I can no longer tolerate it. Do you understand what I'm saying?"

Chase wiped the tear off of his cheek and nodded. "I do."

"I'm going to need more than this from you."

Chase stood and saluted. "If you give me another chance, I'll prove to you that I can be an asset to the Star Alliance. I give you my word."

Tharowni stood from the bench and took a long breath.

"I've done everything I can do for you, and by all rights tonight should have been your last day on this station. Please don't make me regret this."

"I won't."

"You're months away from graduation, but if you keep your nose clean, you'll pass all the tests with flying colors. Of that, I have no doubt. It is highly unlikely you'll ever be given a command, but you're one hell of a pilot, Cadet Athanatos. Don't squander your future, okay?"

"Thank you, Admiral. Believe me, starting now you won't hear a peep out of me in class, and I'll never arrive late again."

"I'll hold you to your word, Cadet. Now go have your face checked out in med-bay and try to get some rest."

～

WHEN CHASE DIDN'T ANSWER his doorbell, he heard the person resort to incessant knocking. While he wasn't in the mood to see anybody, he still opened his quarter's doors. There stood Fillio, smiling at him.

"Mind if I come in?" she asked.

"I'm not sure I'll be good company tonight."

"It's okay. At least you'll have some. Where's your roommate?"

"I don't know where Daniel is."

"So, what happened?"

"They didn't get rid of me, that's what happened."

"Well, thank the Gods of Olympus for that."

"Yeah," said Chase absently.

They talked for a few minutes, during which Chase told Fillio the reason why he still had a chance at graduation.

"You're one lucky ba—" but Fillio caught herself. "You know..." she added.

"I know."

Before he could say another word, her lips were on his, and soon they were intertwined on his bunk bed. Chase lost track of time as they made out for what felt like an eternity. When Fillio's hand traveled south and brushed in between his legs, he caught her hand. They both opened their eyes.

"What's wrong? I thought you'd like us to go a little further tonight, you know, blow off some steam."

Part of Chase wanted nothing more than to do just that. But he knew very well that breaking one more rule was no longer an option. In fact, he shouldn't have made out with Fillio at all.

"I— I'm sorry, but no," he said, trying not to sound too harsh.

"What's wrong?"

"I can't do this."

"That's okay," she said, pulling her hand and going to caress his face instead. "We can just make out tonight."

But when she was about to kiss him, he pulled back.

"I don't think you understand what I'm trying to say. I can't do any of this, not anymore."

Her expression changed. "What are you saying?"

Chase sat on the edge of the bunk bed. "This is against regulations, we shouldn't be involved in this way."

"You've got to be shitting me. Did you get hit hard in the head during the brawl? Because Chase Athanatos citing regulations is kind of ironic. Is that a not so subtle way of telling me you don't like me anymore?"

Chase always enjoyed hanging out with Fillio, but never really felt like his heart belonged to her. If it had, he wouldn't be telling her this.

"No, of course not. My entire life I did anything that I wanted, the more against the flow, the better. I guess it's part of my DNA, but I came within an inch of losing the opportunity of flying tonight. I— I can't continue on this path, or I'll never get my wings."

And I want my wings; I need to fly a starfighter. That much is certain.

Fillio got up and went straight for the door.

"Fillio, don't take it personally," Chase tried to tell her. But she was already gone.

$$5$$

Saroudis gazed at the class for what felt like the longest time.

"Today we'll do live exercises, similar to what we did yesterday, except I want you to fight each other this time, not AI craft. In pairs, so choose your wingmen."

Chase looked at Daniel, who nodded in agreement.

Soon they had attached the neural interface to their temples and were each flying a Manticore starfighter. The HUD overlaid the call signs of the pilots atop their ships, so each pilot knew who they would fight.

"Holy crap," said Daniel.

"What?" asked Chase.

"Look who we're fighting."

Chase looked at the incoming fighters, the names atop the fighters weren't the call signs, but the last names. Saroudis and Tharowni. Chase grinned.

"Daniel, whatever happens, we *have* to win this one."

"I was sure you were gonna say that. How do you want to proceed? They're not exactly rookies, you know."

"I'll take Saroudis. You take the admiral."

"Ok, so no plan whatsoever. Not that I think it would make the slightest bit of difference, either could probably both kick our asses in their sleep."

Not if I have anything to say about it.

"Try and think positively, will ya? You're ruining my buzz."

"Of course I am."

Chase locked onto Saroudis and opened fire. The captain evaded, allowing Chase to get on his six pretty quickly. Chase got a good lock tone and fired up his first missile. Saroudis cut forward thrusters, rotated his ship, kept its current momentum, and took the missile out with laser fire. Some of the shots impacted with Chase's shields, briefly basking the virtual cockpit in bluish light.

Chase wondered why the captain hadn't just deployed countermeasures. Perhaps he wanted to signal to him that he wasn't scared of engaging in a dogfight with Chase, which made this encounter, even if only a simulation, all the more thrilling.

By the time his shield stopped glowing, Saroudis had veered away, but Chase wouldn't let him off the hook so easily, and he re-engaged him, but acquiring another lock proved a more difficult task than dispatching four simultaneous AI ships. This told Chase that it didn't matter how good he was against AI enemies, in the real world he would have to fight fierce adversaries that would not be predictable.

Before he knew it, Chase's aft shield was hit. Tharowni was pounding on them.

"Daniel! What the hell are you doing? I thought you had the admiral."

"Hey, take it easy, I'm trying. I'm on his six, but he's

throwing me off the scent with some pretty fancy old-fart flying."

"Get—him—off my six!" protested Chase.

"Believe me, I'm trying!"

Chase replicated the captain's earlier move, spun his fighter as he killed his forward thrusters, and retaliated against the admiral. He unleashed low-powered high-frequency laser fire to drain Tharowni's shields. The admiral was expertly dodging a good majority, but Chase managed to bring the shields down fifty percent when he locked onto the ship and selected two missiles.

With a good tone, Chase fired them. What happened next he didn't expect. Tharowni instantly deployed a flurry of countermeasures and veered upward. Chase's missiles went forward, taking the countermeasure bait when Daniel's fighter emerged and ran into both. His fighter spun uncontrollably.

Fuck!

"What the hell! Did you just fire at me?" Daniel protested.

"Those were meant for Tharowni."

"That makes me feel *so* much better."

"Head in the game!" Saroudis' voice cracked up over the comms.

Dammit, Sarou—

The distraction had opened up offensive possibilities that Saroudis would not miss. Chase was taking heavy fire from the starboard side. He swore in his mind as he evaded, but Saroudis didn't let him breathe. He fired a couple of missiles, forcing Chase to use countermeasures.

Saroudis was gaining on him; scoring more and more laser hits on his aft shields.

Damn, he's good!

Chase tried every evasive maneuver he could think of to shake Saroudis off his ass, but he kept coming. Chase wished with all his might that he could get his fighter to stop so that Saroudis would overshoot him. Before he could key in the commands, his ship did exactly as he had wished.

What the hell? How's that even possible?

As Saroudis screamed past his canopy, Chase took advantage of the situation and showered the captain's shields with everything he had. What happened, was there a glitch in the simulator? Or had Chase entered his commands without realizing? He really wanted to win this fight, so he decided to let it go, but something smelled fishy.

Saroudis took evasive maneuvers, and Chase followed suit still pounding on his shields.

"Just another few seconds and you're mine," Chase shouted.

But then Daniel's fighter exploded nearby.

Shit!

Tharowni didn't lose time and vectored toward Chase.

This is NOT good!

He had enough trouble just trying to dispatch Saroudis, with the admiral on his way, the situation grew from dire to desperate. For a moment Chase froze, realizing that if that had been a real-life fight, his best friend in the whole world would have been killed. Anger started to make Chase's blood boil.

Saroudis' aft shields were slowly approaching critical, and Chase locked a missile on the captain's tailpipe, but he knew that Saroudis would dodge it, so he prepared a second missile. His instinct told him the captain would break right, so he switched the second missile to manual trajectory and aimed it a little over two points off Saroudis' starboard bow and fired the missiles in quick succession.

Saroudis deployed countermeasures and broke to starboard, his own countermeasure must have masked the second missile from his visuals as he ran into it, which not only finished off his shields but took out one of his engines as the ship spun in space, spewing coolant from a leak.

Chase was about to finish Saroudis off when his locking alarms blared at the incoming four missiles.

"Holy crap! The admiral doesn't want me to win this."

Chase deployed countermeasures, and two of the missiles fell for it, but the other two reacquired Chase's Manticore as they flew through the countermeasure.

Oh, no you don't.

Chase went evasive, veered hard to starboard, and soon was facing the admiral. Chase redistributed power from his shields to the engines to outrun the missiles long enough to execute his next move. He squeezed the trigger and unleashed a barrage of laser fire toward the admiral, pummeling his shield. Tharowni did the same, as he was left with no other choice but to try and shoot down Chase first since the admiral had fired his last remaining missiles.

That mistake would cost him the fight, Chase decided. Both fighters kept advancing toward one another, not even trying to dodge incoming fire, the perfect standoff. Who would blink first?

Chase had no intention to, he had something else in mind. He fired his last missile, knowing that the heavy barrage of laser fire wouldn't get to his target, but he only needed to distract the admiral for a second. The missile screamed toward Tharowni's craft. Midway it got shot down and exploded, and Chase stopped firing his lasers the moment it happened and diverted all weapons and half his shields' power to the thrusters. With his shield's power halved, he redirected all their energy to reinforce the frontal shields only.

That was an all-in move, as the twin missiles, still locked onto his craft, continued to gain on him, but by boosting his engine's power another thirty percent, he could delay their catching up to him for an additional second or two, which was all he needed. He flew through the cloud of flames his exploding missile created, still on a collision course with Tharowni's craft.

"Goodbye, Admiral," Chase said as he turned at the last second just enough to avoid a collision. The pursuing missiles didn't adjust to his last-second maneuvering and continued straight on, impacting with his prey. Tharowni's Manticore exploded into a million pieces.

Chase redistributed power to his shields.

Pride filled his heart, but he knew this battle wasn't over. He looked at his instruments to try and locate Saroudis, who Chase had no doubt had recovered from the damage he had done to his craft earlier. His radar was displaying nothing but noise.

Sneaky, Captain, but that won't save you.

Chase tried acquiring a visual on Saroudis' ship; he maneuvered to try and cover the most angles possible. The captain was nowhere to be seen. He must have been close and was able to compensate for Chase's movements to prevent him from establishing a visual line of sight.

Chase opened a broadband channel.

"You can run, Captain, but you can't hide forever."

"Who says I'm hiding, Cadet? It's game over time. You fought well."

What?

Chase looked to his port side, saw nothing, turned his head to his starboard side, and that's when he saw the incoming fighter, flying as fast as a shooting star. Chase didn't have time to react, and Saroudis' ship crashed into his starboard flank. Both craft exploded, and the simulation ended.

Chase removed the neural link from his temple. He was frustrated but tried not to show it.

"Those were some impressive flight moves you displayed, Cadet," said Saroudis.

"Thank you, Captain. Likewise."

Saroudis nodded. "But you're still dead, and so is your wingman."

"Remember me?" said Daniel.

"Sorry, perhaps I shouldn't have split us up."

"*Perhaps*?" said Tharowni, arching an accusatory eyebrow at Chase.

Chase decided to ignore the admiral and turned his attention back to Saroudis.

"I never expected you to ram into me. But in that scenario you would have died as well, so why do it?"

"First and foremost to teach you a valuable lesson. As for dying, Cadet, I'm a captain, every morning when I put my uniform on, I do it knowing that today may very well be my last day and that I may be required to go down with my ship. I just wanted you to learn that there is such a thing as a no-win situation. I want you to be prepared for it, because as sure as the sun will set on the horizon tomorrow, there will be a time where you'll be faced with such a dilemma."

Chase reflected on those words as he nodded solemnly.

6

It was the middle of the night, and Chase couldn't sleep. He could hear Daniel snoring from the top bunk. In fact, his friend was so loud he felt like he could probably hear him from another galaxy. Chase kept replaying the dogfight with the admiral and the captain in his mind over and over again, wondering what he should have done differently.

He reflected on managing to divert power to his thrusters with such efficiency that the captain shot past him. He still didn't remember actually inputting those commands, yet, they had happened. That was the strangest of feelings. It had felt as if he had ordered his ship to do the maneuver with his mind, and the ship had obeyed.

Chase shook his head.

Nah, that's not possible. I must have acted on instinct and simply didn't realize I was doing it.

The station rocked, and Chase was thrown from his bunk and crashed to the cold, hard floor. Red lights turned on as the alarms started blaring.

"Condition Red, the station is under attack, this is not a drill."

Daniel jumped down from the top bunk and helped Chase get back on his feet.

"What the hell is going on? What are we supposed to do?" Chase asked.

"I would imagine standing fast, we're not commissioned pilots yet. They'll let us know if they need us one way or another."

Chase ran to the viewport in their quarters and looked outside. He saw Obsidian destroyers firing toward the station as the *Destiny* battlegroup, apparently having been taken by surprise, was only now undocking from the station. The nearest ship in Chase's line of sight, the *Medusa*, was drifting away from the station when a flurry of torpedoes impacted it broadside. The destroyer split it two before exploding. The resulting shockwave shook the station so violently that both Chase and Daniel crashed to the floor.

"This isn't good," shouted Chase.

"No shit," said Daniel.

"We gotta do something."

"We have to wait for orders."

The speakers crackled in their room. "All pilots, cadets included, are requested to meet with their commanding offi cers, on the double!"

Finally!

"There are your orders," said Chase as he dressed faster than he ever had before in his life.

UPON ARRIVING at their rally point, and in the midst of the chaos, the first thing that Chase noticed was fear in the admiral's eyes. That made him uneasy. It told Chase that this attack was very serious.

"Listen up, cadets. I can't send you to the frontlines, you're not ready. But I need you to man the turrets, the AI targeting won't cut it. Just put your palm on the turret chair, your identification codes will override the automatic targeting. Give them hell. Go! Now!"

Everyone started running away, but Chase grabbed Daniel by the uniform.

"We're going out there," said Chase to both his friend and commanding officer.

There was no shortage of determination and imperative in Chase's tone.

"No, you're not," argued Tharowni.

"We're not manning some damn turrets, we're going out there and helping Saroudis win this fight."

Tharowni's face hardened.

A nearby explosion sent a bright flashing light through the viewport; the *Sparta* had just been destroyed.

"Listen to me, Cadet, now is not the time to disobey orders."

But Chase was determined.

"They need us out there," he insisted, pointing at the *Sparta*'s smoldering debris. "Please."

Tharowni gave both Daniel and Chase an intense look, mulling over his response. He keyed in some commands on his holo-wrist device.

"I've just temporarily bumped the both of you to acting First Lieutenants, the reserve fighters in bay two will let you fly them out of the dock."

Chase exhaled. "Thank you, Admiral."

"Don't thank me just yet, this might be the last time we speak. Please, come back to the barn safely."

"Will do," said Chase.

Chase could tell Daniel was a little shocked by what was happening. It was easy to see how surreal this all was. The entire situation had that nightmare quality. But the adrenaline in Chase told him how real this all was.

Before Daniel could say another word, Chase grabbed him, and they ran toward the launch bays.

"Let's go, they need us out there," pressured Chase over the comms.

"This is insane," said Daniel from his Manticore's cockpit. "We're just two newbies, with no real combat experience. What sort of difference are we expected to make?"

Oh, we'll make a difference, believe me!

"Suck it up. *This* is what we trained for."

"Trained, yes. But we're just cadets, we're not ready for this."

"Not anymore. You heard the admiral, so consider this your final graduation test if that helps. Are you done with pre-flight?"

"I— I don't know, Chase."

Chase could feel his best friend's fear in every one of the syllables he muttered over the radio. He knew he needed to boost his confidence, or he would freeze out there, and Chase couldn't let that happen.

"Look, if you don't feel like coming, then nobody will think less of you. Myself included. You can still disembark your Manticore and find a turret to man. But wouldn't you want to be in control of your fate? I know you, Daniel, I know you have what it takes to take that fighter into space and help fend off this attack."

Chase took a small pause. "So, are you with me?"

The couple of seconds that Daniel took to answer felt like an eternity.

"I'm with you, Chase. Let's give them hell."

"Now you're talking!"

SAROUDIS SWORE as the *Destiny* shook from the impact of the latest Obsidian torpedoes. They were losing the fight. The Empire had taken them by surprise by not showing on long-range sensors, and by the time the crew had rejoined their respective ships, they were already being pounded upon.

The battlegroup had already lost three ships, putting them at a numerical disadvantage. To add insult to injury, the opposing force was strategically positioned far enough from the station making sure to stay out of range of its big guns.

Admiral Tharowni had fired up the station's thrusters but moving a space station was painfully slow, and the enemy had already shown signs of anticipating the maneuver. Worse yet, the Empire jammed subspace frequencies before even opening fire. Therefore, preventing him and the station from sending a subspace signal in order to get reinforcements in on time.

Things were looking bleak. Saroudis dispatched orders to his crew, providing targeting and assigning priorities. He had also tasked his bridge's chief engineer to locate the source of the jamming; they needed to remove the interference as soon as possible.

Saroudis glimpsed two new small signals coming from Starbase Alpha Three. He pinged the pair of Manticores on his holo-screen and saw their call signs. Firestorm and Scorpion, Chase and Daniel's call signs. Saroudis twitched and opened a channel.

"What the hell are the two of you doing in those fighters?" he asked.

Chase answered.

"Acting First Lieutenants Athanatos and Tharraleos, reporting for duty."

"This is not the time for misplaced heroics, Cadet—First Lieutenants," Saroudis corrected himself. "Trust me you don't want your maiden mission in these circumstances, you'll get yourselves killed."

There was a slight pause.

"Negative, Captain. You need all hands on deck, and we have no intention of dying today."

Defiant to the end, oh well, at least he's consistent.

"If we survive this day, Lieutenant, we'll talk about orders and their function in the Star Alliance."

"I'm looking forward to it, Captain. In the meantime, what do you need us to do?"

Before the captain could answer, his engineer transmitted the coordinates of the jamming ship. The lieutenants were the nearest, and coming late to the party, the enemy had not yet begun to target them. A couple of starfighters were by no means any threat for larger ships, and that's something Saroudis could use. It would put both their lives in jeopardy, but something told Saroudis that if there was anybody that could pull off the move he had in mind, Chase was the one to do it.

"Very well, I'm uploading coordinates; this ship is jamming subspace frequencies, and I need you both to take it out of play."

"Consider it done," said Chase.

"No, no, Lieutenant Athanatos, no bravado, or you'll get

killed. Please use the exact flight plan approach I've uploaded with the coordinates, do not dare deviate from it, or I may blow you to smithereens, and I don't want to have to deal with that kind of paperwork, you feel me?"

"Understood, but why would you blow us up?"

"I'm going to use the *Destiny*'s batteries to cover your approach, that's the only way two measly Manticores can have a shot at doing this. Once you're in range, unload your entire ordnance, don't save anything, alright? Right now you're just a blip on the enemy's scopes, which gives you the element of surprise, they'll never think you'd be mad enough to try and take that ship out."

"With all due respect," said Daniel. "There's no fucking way we can bring that target down, even with all our missiles and torpedoes. Their shields will eat them for breakfast and keep smiling at us."

"I'm well aware of that, Lieutenant, that's why I'll have a full complement of torpedoes take a large bite out of their shields. For this to work, you need to stay on point, follow my instructions, and trust me. Can you do that?"

"I can," said Daniel. "Chase?"

"Sure," said Chase.

"I cannot stress this enough," said Saroudis. "If you deviate from the plan, I'll have to write a eulogy for both your asses and I would just plain hate having to do that."

"Understood," said Chase and Daniel in unison.

7

"Oh, I think I'm going to regret this," Daniel said over the comms.

"No, you won't. Tomorrow we'll look back at this and smile at the whole thing."

Chase and Daniel were sticking to the exact flight path leading them to their targets. Saroudis had not been kidding, the *Destiny* was saturating the area with cover fire, making sure any enemy fighter stupid enough to try and get to them would get obliterated. If either of them made the slightest twitch, they'd suffer the same fate.

A volley of friendly laser fire passed awfully close to both their ships, with a couple of stray shots passing between them.

"Please tell me you're at the very least finding this as unnerving as I am?" asked Daniel.

"Sorry, pal, no can do. This is *fun*, but well, you know me, I live for this shit."

"I was really hoping this crazy-suicidal attitude of yours was just something you brought to the simulator. That once under fire it would get somewhat tamed."

"Who's suicidal? In case I wasn't clear earlier, neither of us are dying today; I'll make it an order if that helps you get it through your thick skull."

"Hey...We're both of the same ranks, so technically you can't order me around. And if one of us is ever making it to Wing Commander, we both know who that will be."

"You'll make a fine Wing Commander, Daniel, of that I have no doubt. But in the meantime, why don't you grow a pair, stop whining, and concentrate on accomplishing our mission. Every one of our friends onboard Starbase Alpha Three is depending on us. If we fail, they could all be killed."

"No pressure, then."

"Just another day in service to the Star Alliance."

They were approaching firing range. The target ship, a massive corvette that kept growing in size as every second passed, opened up on them with long-range artillery. Some of the shots exploded too close for comfort, rocking their ships and lowering their shields little by little.

"Redistribute power to your shields, you can even divert some power from life support," said Chase.

"Did you ever ask yourself why they call it life support? That's because you bloody need the damn thing, Chase!"

"Not all of it, what good will your oxygen be if your shields aren't strong enough to deflect some of that heavy fire?"

"Hard to argue with your logic," conceded Daniel as he mumbled something incomprehensible afterward.

"Alright, we've just entered firing range."

"Locking all ordnance on the target. Ready to fire."

"Don't shoot just yet!" exclaimed Chase.

"What? We have to, Chase. Saroudis said to follow his plan to a T. We have to shoot now!"

"No, we don't. Just trust me on this one, if we shoot now, we'll miss the mark. I've got a visual on the *Destiny*'s torpedoes, they're late to the party, we need another few seconds."

Three rather sizable explosions rocked both their ships heavily.

"Screw this, you're going to get us killed!"

"No, I won't, Daniel. Get ready, in three, two, one...*Fire!*"

Chase and Daniel unleashed all their ordnance in concert toward the enemy corvette and veered to starboard shortly after. A total of eight missiles and four torpedoes left the Manticore wings and screamed toward the target. Meanwhile, the *Destiny*'s torpedoes were on course, all targeting the same area for maximum effect. They impacted and lit up the corvette's shields. Chase and Daniel's missiles were next, which smashed into the still lit-up shields, but they seemed to hold.

"Shit, it's not working!" exclaimed Daniel.

"Have faith, brother."

The first Manticore torpedo exploded on the enemy, and the remaining three passed through their shields, resulting in a trio of large explosions that split it in half.

"See, I told you it would work."

Daniel swore. "I hate it when you're right."

"Get used to it, bro, I'm always right."

"And so fucking modest."

Chase chuckled. "Yeah, that too."

SAROUDIS WAS ONLY HALF surprised when the corvette exploded. Not that he didn't trust his plan or the newbies to deliver. During his time with the cadets in the classroom, he had sensed both of them had great, if diametrically different, flight skills.

Daniel was a by the book, straight as an arrow, grade-A student, and Chase...well, Chase was a crazy-genius type. Both useful in a multitude of situations. But they had managed to follow their orders and even compensated for an involuntary delay in the firing of the *Destiny*'s torpedoes.

Impressive.

"Get Star Alliance headquarters on the line this instant, request any ship in the area to assist, and have them send the entire second fleet if they have to!" ordered Saroudis.

"Distress call sent," answered the comm officer.

Meanwhile, Saroudis opened a channel to the heroes of the hour.

"Well done, Firestorm and Scorpion, now go back to the barn."

"Understood, Captain. Thank you," said Daniel.

"Mmmm...that's a negative on your last order, this battle isn't over," said Chase.

Saroudis shook his head.

"Listen, Son, I like you, but this is not how things are done in the service."

"I understand that, Captain, but you need us."

"This war needs good pilots, alive. You don't have any missiles left, and you're about to catch the kind of aggro you don't want to deal with. Do you get my drift, Lieutenant?"

"We still have laser cannons, which means we're prepped and ready to dispatch enemy starfighters, sir."

Saroudis stared stoically at his tactical holo-display, slowly stroking the bottom of his beard.

"I'll only agree to let you in this fight if you're both in agreement on this."

There was a pause.

"Daniel?" inquired Chase.

"Lieutenant Athanatos is correct, sir. We still have cannons."

Saroudis could tell Daniel was not exactly thrilled but his allegiance to his friend, especially under the circumstances, was commendable.

"Very well, then. I'm sending you a list of enemy targets to engage."

"Consider them history," said Chase.

I guess we're about to find out if Chase is as brilliant as he is insane.

No matter the case, Saroudis had to admit that he respected the enthusiasm and courage under fire. Especially when considering that this was their first taste of war. Saroudis' gut told him that it wouldn't be their last.

Chase smiled as he blew up a third Obsidian starfighter in the last five minutes of engagement. He was running on thrills and adrenaline and loving every second of it. Part of him had wondered if his instincts would be as sharp in space as they were in the simulator. And he was surprised to see that they seemed to be even sharper with the threat of impending death weighing upon him.

"Nice shot!" exclaimed Daniel.

"Thanks, bro. Watch your six, you've got incoming."

"I see him, let's take that one together, shall we?"

"Gladly."

"I'll get it to engage me and deliver it to you on a silver platter, just don't let him shoot me out of the sky before then, please?"

"You got it."

Daniel waited until the Obsidian bogey was on his tail to go evasive. He managed to dodge most of the shots and brought the enemy craft to Chase's vicinity. Chase engaged the enemy with successive laser fire, draining its shields rapidly. If he had missiles left, now would have been a perfect time to fire one, but instead, he waited until the enemy's aft shields were down and switched to supercharged laser shots and sent a volley of them toward the target.

Bull's-eye. The shots impacted with one of the ship's engines and sent the fighter into a wild spin.

"Dan, finish him off, there are three more ships incoming. I don't want them to catch us with our pants down. Rejoin me once you're done."

"I don't like these odds, perhaps we shouldn't split up."

"We'll be fine."

Chase veered away and saw Daniel arc back toward the damaged enemy ship, he re-engaging and blowing it out of the sky before vectoring back toward Chase. By that time, the three enemy fighters had entered firing range and wasted no time showering Chase's ship with heavy laser fire. Chase went evasive as best as he could, wishing he still had missiles.

"I'm going to get them to follow me, make sure you reduce their numbers with your first pass, otherwise I'm history."

"Please don't say things like that."

"Ready?"

"Be careful. Ready."

Chase smiled as he shot laser fire toward the incoming bogeys before breaking off, making sure to get their attention. As planned, they kept formation as they attempted to lock onto Chase. It took some pretty fancy flying to make sure they couldn't get a missile lock. Meanwhile, Daniel engaged one of the fighters, but then it disengaged and broke off formation.

"Stay on the pair," said Chase, "we'll get that one later."

"Roger that."

Daniel lit up the second fighter hard. Soon, its shield went down. A few more shots blew it to kingdom come. He started pounding on the remaining fighter. But that one was avoiding incoming fire with much more efficiency, all the while managing to score hits on Chase's aft shields.

"Get this fucker off my six, will ya?"

"I'm trying."

"Try harder."

"Not helping, Chase! He's as annoying as you when it comes to crazy flying."

"Was there a compliment somewhere in there?"

"Screw that, Chase, I'm serious, he's bringing down your shields faster than I'm impacting his."

"Fuck!"

Before Daniel could inquire about his friend's swearing, he saw two missiles leave the enemy's craft and sail toward Chase. Daniel reacted on instinct, disengaged the enemy, vectored hard to the side to get a better line of sight, and opened fire on the missiles.

He got one pretty quickly but missed the second one, impacting Chase's shield instead.

"Sorry about that, bro!"

"Thanks for the assist but re-engage this sucker, please. I've got an idea."

Daniel re-engaged the Obsidian fighter.

"Understood. Wanna keep me in the loop?"

"It's going to be pretty self-explanatory."

Chase got rid of the incoming missile by deploying

countermeasures with perfect timing. Then he slowed his Manticore down. Daniel had witnessed Chase doing this many times in simulation, or so Daniel hoped, as Chase cut power to the forward engines and reversed thrusters at maximum. The pursuing craft didn't expect the maneuver, and before he knew it, he now had both Chase and Daniel on his six.

Chase came so close to Daniel's wing that they could literally wave at each other from their respective canopies. They looked at each other.

"You're crazy," said Daniel. "I never thought this would ever work outside of the simulator."

"When will you learn to trust me," Chase said, a big smile spreading across his face. "Now, let's blow this asshole to bits."

They both rained down their laser fire, and while the pilot was extremely skilled at evasive maneuvers, he couldn't dodge them both. Eventually, its shields went down and both Daniel and Chase's lasers simultaneously impacted with its hull, turning the Obsidian ship into a fireball before it disintegrated completely.

"Who's getting credit for that kill?" asked Daniel.

"You can have this one, brother."

"I don't need your charit—"

But then something went terribly wrong. Daniel was hit with a missile coming out of nowhere and spun uncontrollably.

"Daniel!!"

8

———

Daniel's ship spun so wildly it impacted with Chase's. Both their shields lit up, but Chase was able to regain control quickly. Daniel wasn't so lucky.

"Talk to me, Daniel?"

"I'm hit! One of my engines is acting up, I can't seem to get out of the spin. Shit!"

"What?"

"That motherfucker has locked another missile on me."

"Hang on tight."

"Well, you'd better do one of your magic tricks 'cause there's no way I can get rid of that missile. I'll be lucky if I don't pass out. The damn engines won't let me get out of this spin."

"I got your back. Turn off your engines now and reactivate them full burn when I tell you."

"Turn my engines off? What for?"

"Just do what I say."

"Roger that," said Daniel.

His engines died off, and the ship continued to spin.

Chase had to act fast as he would only have one shot at this. He diverted all the power he could from secondary systems to the thrusters and shield and vectored straight for Daniel at max burn.

"I think I'm gonna be sick," said Daniel.

Hang on my friend, I'm coming. With any luck, I won't blow us both up.

Chase almost froze at the thought. His best friend's life was on the line. If his crazy idea didn't pan out, would he be able to live with the consequences of his actions? Fear started to creep into Chase's heart. But then he heard the sweet female voice again in his mind.

Trust your instincts, Chase, they never fail you.

Chase was a little worried about hearing voices, but perhaps his subconscious was telling him to hold to his guns. He wondered why it would address him as a female, but right now he couldn't worry about that.

"Alright, I'm going to graze you ever so slightly."

"You're going to do *what*? Have you lost all your marbles?"

"I know what I'm doing."

"Alright," he said, with doubt creeping into his voice.

"Activate your engines at full burn on my mark."

"Standing by."

Chase's instincts told him what trajectory to take to generate enough force on his fly-by to mitigate Daniel's current spin and allow him to regain control of his fighter. Of course, that was half the battle, there was still a missile on approach. He needed to take care of that as well. A quick glance at his instruments also allowed him to keep an eye on the enemy ship that had fired the missile; if he survived the next part, they'd have to take care of it too.

As Daniel's ship got bigger on his visuals, Chase took a deep breath and held his breath.

"Mark!" he shouted.

Chase saw Daniel's engines powering up as he reached his position a fraction of a second before the missile, which was locked and ready to claim his best friend's life. The moment Chase grazed Daniel's Manticore, the missile locked onto his engines because Daniel's weren't emitting enough energy, and Chase had passed right into the trajectory of the missile, forcing it to follow him.

Daniel's engines took a second to power up to full burn, but by then both Chase and the missile were gone and grazing his shields with Daniel's had stabilized Daniel's spin enough that when the engine kicked off, he managed to get out of the spin.

Chase let the air trapped in his lungs escape as his comms crackled.

"You're one crazy-talented pilot, thanks for saving my hide. I wish I could say I would have done the same if our positions had been reversed...but—"

Chase didn't even understand how his brain could show him what to do in these situations, he was acting on pure instinct and had learned to trust it over the years. It had yet to fail him.

"You're welcome, Dan. While I do appreciate the intention, we both know that if our situations had been reversed, you'd just have killed the both of us a second before the missile hit."

Daniel chuckled. "Ouch. But probably true."

Chase still had to get rid of the missile gaining on him. Fortunately, he was flying at max burn when he deliberately confused the missile to follow him instead of his friend. But he only had a handful of seconds to get rid of it before he was blown to pieces. The near miss maneuver to save Daniel had lowered his shields enough that he wasn't sure he would survive the impact. Not that he had ever planned to let that missile ever hit his Manticore.

Chase vectored toward the fighter that had launched the missile in the first place with a vengeance and activated a short-range jamming field. For his plan to work, he would need the enemy pilot's instruments to go blind.

I'll teach you to try and kill my friends. Pray to whatever gods you believe in.

Chase aligned his Manticore on a collision course with the enemy and opened fire with his lasers, scoring hit after hit on its frontal shields. The Obsidian fighter did the same, but Chase put his fighter into a variable barrel roll to dodge a good half of the incoming fire. His shields still lit up every other second.

When they grew closer, Chase deployed countermeasures, with the missile so close to his Manticore now he knew there was almost no way they would work, but he needed to distract the opposing pilot more than the missile itself. Chase then veered away, feinting to break the standoff, hoping it would keep the Obsidian pilot on his course for just another second or two. And, it did.

With Chase's countermeasures dying off, the pilot never saw his missile come back. It impacted with the already lowered bogeys shields and tore the ship to shreds.

"You'll have to teach me that one," said Daniel as Chase disabled the jamming field.

"Not sure I can teach you how my gut works, but we'll figure something out. Now, get back to the barn, your ship is too damaged to stay in the fight."

"I think I can hold her together."

Chase looked at his instruments and checked the status of Daniel's ship.

"That's a negative, you barely have any shields, and you're leaking power like there's no tomorrow. At this rate, you'll be out of juice before you can return to the starbase."

"Right. What about an escort?"

While Chase liked the idea of returning to the starbase, ending a successful run on multiple kills, the battle wasn't over. Saroudis might still need his help. He decided to compromise.

"I'll cover you until you're out of range of enemy fire."

"Fair enough. Thanks, Chase."

"Don't mention it."

Soon, Daniel was out of danger, and Chase veered back toward the battlefield. He opened a channel to Saroudis on the *Destiny*.

"What's the status, Captain? Where do you need me?"

"Reinforcements are five minutes away, I think we can hold them o—"

But static interfered with the comm channel as an enemy ship exploded in close range to the *Destiny*.

"Captain! Have you been hit? Captain, please respond."

Chase had trouble breathing as he looked at his scopes and saw that the *Destiny* had lost its starboard shields. He adjusted his vector and pushed his ship's thrusters to their maximum limits.

9

———

"*Destiny*, come in," said Chase.

The *Destiny*'s deck lights flickered madly, which was not a good sign. The remaining enemy destroyer on the *Destiny*'s starboard side launched three torpedoes. The ship was far enough away for Chase to try and intercept one or two of them, but he knew in his heart that he would never be able to shoot three of them in time.

"Chase Athanatos to Star Alliance fighters, there are three torpedoes on course to the *Destiny*. Its starboard shields are down. Can you help me intercept?"

"This is Alpha Three, I'm close enough to try but I can't shak—"

Static replaced the pilot's voice, and his Manticore faded from Chase's scope.

Dammit!

"No risk, no glory."

Chase's Manticore screamed past the *Destiny*'s belly, plunging Chase's cockpit into darkness for half a second. He had visuals on the incoming torpedoes, aligned with the first one, and opened fire with low-power, high-rate lasers. The goal here was to impact a small target and let its own contact sensors do the rest. The faster the rate of fire, the better.

It only took two seconds of sustained fire for Chase to detonate the first bogey. He had hoped the explosion would set off the other two torpedoes on course to the disabled *Destiny*, but no such luck.

Chase quickly scanned his instruments to choose his next target, looking at possible impacts from the torpedoes to see which one of them could create the most damage if the *Destiny*'s shields didn't get back up in time, which was more than probable. The missile on his farthest starboard side was the winner. A direct impact on the *Destiny* could light up its landing bays and create secondary explosions.

Chase lit it up with everything he had but didn't manage to get it on his first pass. He cut thrusters, swiveled his ship, and re-engaged them at full power the moment he was done with the maneuver, all the while firing at the torpedo. A couple of hits grazed it, but the torpedo stayed on course.

He needed to make a decision and fast. If both of them impacted with the ship, the *Destiny* could be destroyed. His mind raced to try and find a solution when he remembered his simulation engagement with Saroudis and the no-win scenario. He never thought he'd be faced with it so soon.

Chase siphoned all the power from every system on the ship, except for minimal life support and low-power communications, and fed the extra power to the thrusters. Every holo-instrument in his cockpit turned off, plunging him into solitary darkness. The Manticore flew without shields and no weapons, but it flew faster than the torpedoes, fast enough to catch one of them before it impacted.

For a second he thought that perhaps if he set his ship

on the right trajectory and ejected, then he would survive. But that was wishful thinking, he couldn't risk missing his mark, and even if he did hit his ship after ejecting, the high-yield torpedo's explosion would incinerate him just the same.

Never thought this is how I would go out.

Chase was a few seconds away from his target. His thoughts went to his best friend, Daniel. Perhaps it had been a mistake to send him back to the barn. Maybe together they could have found another way. It mattered not anymore. He couldn't let the crew of the *Destiny* die, not if there was anything he could do about it. Chase took a long breath.

Goodbye, Daniel.

Just before he was about to impact with the torpedo, he saw a missile trail impact with the other torpedo a few klicks from his position. His comms crackled to life.

"Chase! Break off now!"

It was Fillio's voice. Chase broke away from the torpedo, and Fillio waited a second before blasting it with another missile. The resulting shockwave shook Chase's Manticore and sent him into a spin, but he managed to recover.

"Holy crap, I thought my number was up. Not to sound ungrateful, but what are you doing out here?"

"Well, for one, saving your ass, but I just thought it unfair that the two of you got to go out and play with the big guys, so I convinced Tharowni to let me take a reserve fighter."

"I'm glad you did. Thank you, Fillio."

Chase felt both relieved and guilty. He had basically broken up with her, and now she was saving his life. Hopefully, one day he could repay her for that.

"Chase, I still have four torpedoes on my bird, I decided

to take a strike loadout, what do you say we blow that ship to smithereens before it reloads its torpedo tubes?"

"Sounds like a plan, but I only have lasers. If you think your ordnance is enough to take it, I can try and cover you."

"Lasers won't make a dent, but that destroyer's shields are in bad shape. I suggest you boost your shields to the max and provide its laser battery with a diversion. I'll do the rest."

"Sounds like a plan."

A couple more starfighters joined their wings.

"Alpha Two and Six to Starbase fighters, thank you for saving our ship. Do you require assistance?"

"Hello, boys," said Fillio playfully, "if you could help my friend here clear a path to that destroyer, and if you happen to have any torpedoes left, we could use that too."

"I'm all out," answered Alpha Three. "Six?"

"I have one left and two missiles. I can slave their targeting and release to your fighter."

"Neat, I'll take it, thank you. Six is it?"

"Lieutenant Commander Kal Maniakos. They call me Maniac."

"Nice to make your acquaintance, Maniac. Acting Lieutenant Fillio Steriopoulou. You can call me Seraph."

Alpha Three, Six, and Chase teamed up to clear a path for Fillio's Manticore until it reached firing range. She kept her approach vector for another few klicks as she wanted to release her payload at an optimum distance. When she and Six finally fired, Chase was already veering away. His power nodes were severely damaged, the resultant shockwave from the destroyer blowing up would render his fighter completely inoperable.

When the payload hit the shields of the Obsidian destroyer, it lit the dark space with a very bright, temporarily blinding flash. The ship had been obliterated, turned to space dust.

Multiple flashes lit up the area in the distance as Star Alliance reinforcements jumped into the war theater. Unsurprisingly, what was left of the Obsidian Empire forces turned tail and jumped away.

We've won.

The comms came to life with Saroudis' voice.

"Thank you all for protecting the *Destiny*. We came close to losing her. Even though we've won the battle, this has been a tragic day with the loss of both the *Medusa* and the *Sparta*. But for now, let's just be happy this engagement is over. All fighters, return to base."

Chase could feel the strain in the captain's voice, how heavily the loss of life today had impacted Saroudis. Chase wondered if one day he would be in a position where thousands of lives would depend on his choices. He did not relish the thought and preferred discarding it altogether.

10

———

"Were you really going to sacrifice yourself?" asked Daniel on their way to cargo bay three.

"I didn't think I had a choice, you know," answered Chase. "If I didn't, and people died, I would never have forgiven myself."

"I know, and I think if I were in your shoes, I would have done the same, but boy, that's heavy. Our first mission and we both came within a hairsbreadth from dying. Makes you think, doesn't it?"

"That's what we're fighting for. For the freedom and safety of the Star Alliance, to oppose the tyranny of the Empire, and at the end of the day, for one another."

"Well said. I must admit I'm no longer in a hurry to graduate. I mean...today was filled with enough excitement to last me for the next few months of class."

I wish I could get back in the cockpit right this instant myself.

Chase simply nodded.

"Do we know why we've been called to the cargo bay?" asked Daniel.

"I have no clue."

When Daniel and Chase stepped in, the first thing they noticed was the crowd of pilots and other officers neatly lined up. They heard running footsteps behind them, and Fillio came in between them and put her hands around both their necks.

"Do you think they'll give us medals?" she asked.

Medals?

"I— I didn't consider that..." said Chase.

"I don't think that's why we're here, but that would be cool, wouldn't it?" said Daniel.

Fillio exhaled loudly. "You two are good pilots, but you're not the brightest, are you?"

They advanced toward the rest of the pilots who split into two groups, making a path in the middle for Chase, Daniel, and Fillio to walk through.

Saroudis was waiting with Admiral Tharowni on the other side. Tharowni's voice boomed through the cargo bay's speakers.

"All hands, salute!"

Oh shit, she's right. We're getting medals.

They were amazed at what was happening to them. The smiles, gratitude, and admiration from their fellow pilots filled their hearts with pride. It all felt surreal. When they arrived at the front of the podium, Saroudis addressed the crowd.

"These three cadets have displayed incredible courage under fire today. Even though they haven't officially graduated from the Star Alliance Flight Academy, when danger beckoned, they answered the call of their hearts and risked their lives for our values. It is with great pride and honor that I bestow upon them the Wings of Valor for extreme courage and bravery."

Saroudis pinned a set of quadrinium-enhanced metal wings on each of them and saluted.

The trio of cadets saluted back as the crowd applauded. A tremendous sense of pride filled Chase's heart. Not too long ago he had almost been dismissed from the academy, something that would have broken his heart. But now, he truly felt like his life was back on track.

LATER THAT DAY, they all celebrated at the mess hall. They were bought many drinks, more than they could handle.

"Boy, what a day," said Chase, raising his glass.

"I'll drink to that," said Fillio.

"So will I," added Daniel.

Admiral Tharowni came to their table.

"Well done, you three. I'm glad you all came back alive from this ordeal, and I will deny it to my grave if you repeat this, but you made me very proud."

"Thank you, Admiral," said Daniel.

"Will you join us," said Chase, pointing at all the drinks. "We could use the help."

The admiral nodded and took a nearby chair to sit with his pupils.

"Did you know that you're the first cadets in history to receive Wings of Valor?" he said.

"Get out of here!" said Chase.

"I'm serious, we don't usually let cadets out of the academy to fly in deadly combat situations, you know. I'm glad you convinced me to let you do this. Things might have turned out very differently otherwise." The admiral's face hardened somewhat. "We could all have been killed today. That was a close call."

"We're still here, so let's celebrate, shall we?" said Fillio getting up.

"Where are you going?" asked Chase.

"Lieutenant Commander Maniakos owes me a drink," she said, winking at Chase.

Good for you, maybe he can give you what I can't, though if he's serious about keeping his job, that shouldn't happen.

"Have fun, say hi to Maniac for us," said Chase.

"Who's Maniac?" asked Daniel.

"That's the lieutenant commander's call sign."

"Oh...peculiar call sign."

"Yeah, 'cause Scorpion isn't?"

"Who calls himself Firestorm?"

"Well, at least mine is accurate."

They both laughed.

Chase and Daniel got up as Captain Saroudis approached the table.

"At ease, you're not on duty at the moment."

"We're not on duty, period," said Chase not even trying to hide the disappointment behind his words.

"We'll be soon enough," said Daniel. "It's our last year at the academy."

Admiral Tharowni smiled.

"I think the captain wants a word with you two. I, for one, will get some rest. Unlike certain people at this table, I actually have class tomorrow. Good night, party well tonight, tomorrow is another day."

It took Chase a while to compute what the admiral meant because, at first, it didn't make any sense. Daniel arrived there faster.

"He's not serious?" he asked Saroudis.

"Please, sit," the captain gestured to the both of them.

They sat back, their looks serious.

"Nothing's official yet, and you may not like the idea. But Admiral Tharowni thinks you will, obviously."

Chase started to feel his heart beat so hard, he thought it was trying to burst out of his chest. Excitement tingled the rest of his body. And even though he thought he knew what was coming next, he still couldn't believe it, so he asked for confirmation.

"What's the idea?"

Saroudis looked straight at Chase.

"I lost two pilots in Alpha squadron, today. If you guys would like your temporary ranks to become official and be First Lieutenants under my command, I'd like to have you on board the *Destiny*."

"Count me in," said Chase with no shortage of pride.

"Me too, Captain, thank you," said Daniel.

"We'll still have to discuss your blatant disregard for the chain of command, Lieutenant Athanatos, but seeing as if you hadn't disobeyed a direct order, we might not all be sitting here enjoying each other's company. I've decided to leave that part out of my report. I think it's only fair. Let's just not make a habit of it in the future, though. Can you live with that?"

"Absolutely, Captain."

"Then I'll see you onboard the *Destiny* tomorrow, 0800 sharp. We're to return to Alpha Prime, effect repairs, and replenish this battlegroup with two new ships fresh out of space dock. I suggest you say goodbye to your friends tonight, there's no telling the next time you'll see them. Enjoy the rest of your evening. I'll see you both tomorrow."

They both stayed silent for a few minutes after the captain had left, still reflecting on what had just happened.

"Are we dreaming?" asked Chase.

"Nah...this doesn't feel like a dream; there would be naked chicks if it were."

Chase grinned. "Classy, Dan, classy."

I'm actually a pilot, on board a carrier ship. I can't believe it.

EPILOGUE

A lizard-like Zarlack entered the ready room.

"Report," came a cold voice from the throne.

"I'm afraid I'm the bearer of bad news. The attack on Starbase Alpha Three was lost by the Obsidian Empire."

"As I suspected. Very well, you're dismissed."

The lizard-man bowed, but before turning away, he dared speak again. Something very few in his position would attempt.

"I'm sorry, Master. But I don't understand why you asked me to arrange for the fake intel to be delivered to the Empire. Obviously, you wanted them to attack the station, but you don't seem disappointed that the starbase survived. Have I missed something?"

That was one brave Zarlack. The Master, his face hidden behind a cloak, had beheaded subordinates for less than a stray look, let alone curiosity. Fortunately for this particular Zarlack, he felt magnanimous today.

"It is not your place nor your duty to try and understand

my reasoning. As a matter of fact, I'd encourage you not to continue doing it in the future. While I have no need to tell you this, I'm in a rather good mood at the moment, so I'll tell you this much: I wanted to test a theory and witness how it played out. I'm actually very satisfied with the outcome. I'll look forward to checking the battle logs in more detail."

"I'll have them transmitted to your throne holo-storage at once, Master," said the Zarlack with a bow.

"I can sense you still have questions on the matter. May I suggest you empty your mind of such concerns at once," he said as both his eyes glowed red. "That is unless you'd like me to empty it for you. Which right now is more than a little tempting. Leave, now!"

The imposing scaled creature had a hard time concealing his trembling as a result of his master's words. He bowed respectfully and hastily left the ready room.

Mindless and useless cold-blooded slaves. I look forward to the day I don't have to tolerate their kind any longer.

He knew that the lizard-men species was a means to an end. But that didn't mean he had to enjoy their presence. Nonetheless, for the time being, he needed an army to do his bidding.

The holo-console built in his throne room chair beeped, informing him that he had received the detailed log of the engagement between the Obsidian Empire and the Star Alliance. He sifted through the holo-vids and paused at a couple of starfighters leaving Starbase Alpha Three. He grabbed the small holo-feed with his hands and threw it forward, effectively expanding the holo-feed to the entire room.

There you are, his gaze locked onto Chase's Manticore as he resumed the holo-vid in accelerated mode, focusing only on that fighter throughout the entire battle.

Once he had reviewed the entire footage, he turned the holo-vids off. The Obsidian Empire hadn't exactly impressed him much in this battle, but they could still be useful in the future. Just like the Zarlacks, they would have a small role to play in his plans. There was still much to do before he needed to approach them, however. The Zarlacks hadn't built nearly enough ships to be the reckoning force he needed them to be.

Patience wasn't exactly his strong suit, but he knew very well that rushing unprepared could have dire consequences.

A hiss in a jar next to his throne broke him out of his current thought pattern. He smiled as he lifted the lid off the archaic-looking jar and two yellow eyes glowed in the darkness within. He released the handle, and the cover hovered where it stood, he then presented his forearm to the hissing creature.

The Kyrian snake leaped forward and planted its long fangs into his flesh, releasing its sweet poison into his bloodstream. The burning sensation was almost immediately replaced by a dizzying high. His pupils dilated, and as the snake released his prey and retracted back into the jar, he let himself relax on his throne.

Whether an hour or half a day passed by the time he came back to his senses, he wasn't sure. Not that it mattered to him. The Kyrian snakebite could most certainly kill most species. But he wasn't like the others in this galaxy, and the bite never threatened his life.

Using the Kyrian snake venom was his way of relaxing from the daily stress, as well as a way to cope with old demons haunting him. Late at night, he dreamed about the events that got him here.

I should have killed him when I had the chance. But death is too sweet a release. He needs to suffer; he needs to see everything he holds dear crumble before his eyes.

—== THE END ==—

The story continues in Earth - Last Sanctuary.

ALSO BY CHRISTIAN KALLIAS

—== Access All my Books Here ==—

christiankallias.com

The Universe in Flames Series

- Book 1: Earth - Last Sanctuary (Definitive Edition)
- Book 1.5: Ryonna's Wrath (Novella)
- Book 2: Fury to the Stars
- Book 3: Destination Oblivion
- Book 4: The Beginning of the End
- Book 5: Rise of the Ultra Fury
- Book 6: Shadows of Olympus

- Book 7: Armageddon Unleashed
- Book 8: Twilight of the Gods
- Book 9: Requiem of Souls
- Book 10: To End All Wars (Final Chapter)
- Book 11: Nemesis
- Book 12: Unleashed
- Book 13: Reckoning
- Book 14: Dominion
- Book 15: Fireborn (releases October 2021)
- *Books 1-13 also available in trilogies format.*

Universe In Flames - Origins

- Episode 1: Course Correction
- Episode 2: Damocles Fall
- Wings of Destiny (*this book*)

Far Beyond Series

- Book 0: Across the Galactic Pond
- Book 1: Fire At Will
- Book 2: Make it So!
- Book 3: Battlestations
- *The complete series is available in a box set with an extra story (Book 2.5) called Red Alert.*

Rewind Series

- Book 0: Out of Time (Collateral Damage anthology)
- Book 1: Freedom's End
- Book 2: Pandemonium
- Book 3: Nightfall

- **Galactic Tales** (10 Epic Stories from Earth & Beyond)

Sign up for my newsletter to keep up to date with new releases and promotions.

THANKS TO ALL MY PATRONS

Special thanks to the following people (Destroyer Captain & higher tiers) for supporting my work on Patreon:

Daniel Perret, Lain Laing, Cedric Perret, Michael Slezak, Kevin Moore, Alexander Dodge, Thomas Sipin, M.J. Smith, Richard Hotham, David Stewardson, John Gill, Kell Vagtholm, Nicholas Lepisto, Marc Maillard, Thomas Sipin, Kevin Moore, Sandro Cherubini.

—== Join me on PATREON ==—

https://www.patreon.com/ChristianKallias

ABOUT THE AUTHOR

Christian Kallias is a Bestselling, Award-winning Science Fiction author. He writes Science Fiction Space Opera with a Mythology twist and Fantasy influences.

—== Join me on PATREON ==—

Find me on GoodReads
Follow me on BookBub
Follow me on Facebook
Follow me on Twitter

Keep in touch
www.christiankallias.com
christian@kallias.com